The Pop Duet

Level 3E

Written by Deborah Chancellor
Illustrated by Alex Paterson

What is synthetic phonics?

Synthetic phonics teaches children to recognise the sounds of letters and to blend (synthesise) them together to make whole words.

Understanding sound/letter relationships gives children the confidence and ability to read unfamiliar words, without having to rely on memory or guesswork; this helps them progress towards independent reading.

Did you know? Spoken English uses more than 40 speech sounds. Each sound is called a *phoneme*. Some phonemes relate to a single letter (d-o-g) and others to combinations of letters (sh-ar-p). When a phoneme is written down it is called a *grapheme*. Teaching these sounds, matching them to their written form and sounding out words for reading is the basis of synthetic phonics.

Consultant

I love reading phonics has been created in consultation with
language expert Abigail Steel. She has a background
in teaching and teacher training and is a respected
expert in the field of Synthetic Phonics. Abigail Steel is
a regular contributor to educational publications. Her
international education consultancy supports parents
and teachers in the promotion of literacy skills.

Reading tips

This book focuses on the sounds:
ue as in 'cue'

Tricky words in this book

• Any words in bold may have unusual spellings or are new and have not yet been introduced.

> ### Tricky words in this book:
>
> **out car park to no me wants star are argue here go be you quite**

Extra ways to have fun with this book

• After the reader has read the story, ask them questions about what they have just read:

How did Jess and Zack travel to perform the duet?
Why was Jess sad in the middle of the story?

This way to rock 'n' roll stardom for Jess and Zack!

A pronunciation guide

This grid contains the sounds used in the story and a guide on how to say them.

s as in sat	a as in ant	t as in tin	p as in pig	i as in ink
n as in net	c as in cat	e as in egg	h as in hen	r as in rat
m as in mug	d as in dog	g as in get	o as in ox	u as in up
l as in log	f as in fan	b as in bag	j as in jug	v as in van
w as in wet	z as in zip	y as in yet	k as in kit	qu as in quick
x as in box	ff as in off	ll as in ball	ss as in kiss	zz as in buzz
ck as in duck	pp as in puppy	nn as in bunny	rr as in arrow	gg as in egg
dd as in daddy	bb as in chubby	tt as in attic	sh as in shop	ch as in chip
th as in them	th as in the	ng as in sing	nk as in sunk	le as in bottle
ai as in rain	ee as in feet	ie as in pies	oa as in oak	ue as in cue

Be careful not to add an 'uh' sound to 's', 't', 'p', 'c', 'h', 'r', 'm', 'd', 'g', 'l', 'f' and 'b'. For example, say 'fff' not 'fuh' and 'sss' not 'suh'.

Jess **wants to be** a pop **star**.

"Can **you** sing a duet with **me**?"
she asks Zack.

Zack groans. "Buzz off!" he says.
"Duets **are no** fun!"

Jess and Zack **argue**, but Jess gets her way.

Zack agrees to sing a duet at a pop gig.

The pop gig is at a big venue.

Jess and Zack **go** by bus
to the venue.

The bus runs **out** of fuel on
the way. It stops in a **car park**.

Jess and Zack are stuck.

They can't get to the venue.

Jess is **quite** sad. She still wants
to sing her duet.

Zack **fixes** things.

"Let's sing the duet **here**," he says.

The duet is a hit.

The kids on the bus **cheer**.

"This duet is cool!" they say.

Jess and Zack sing the duet again.

"We don't need a posh venue!"
Jess cries.

"I think duets are fun after all!"
Zack says.

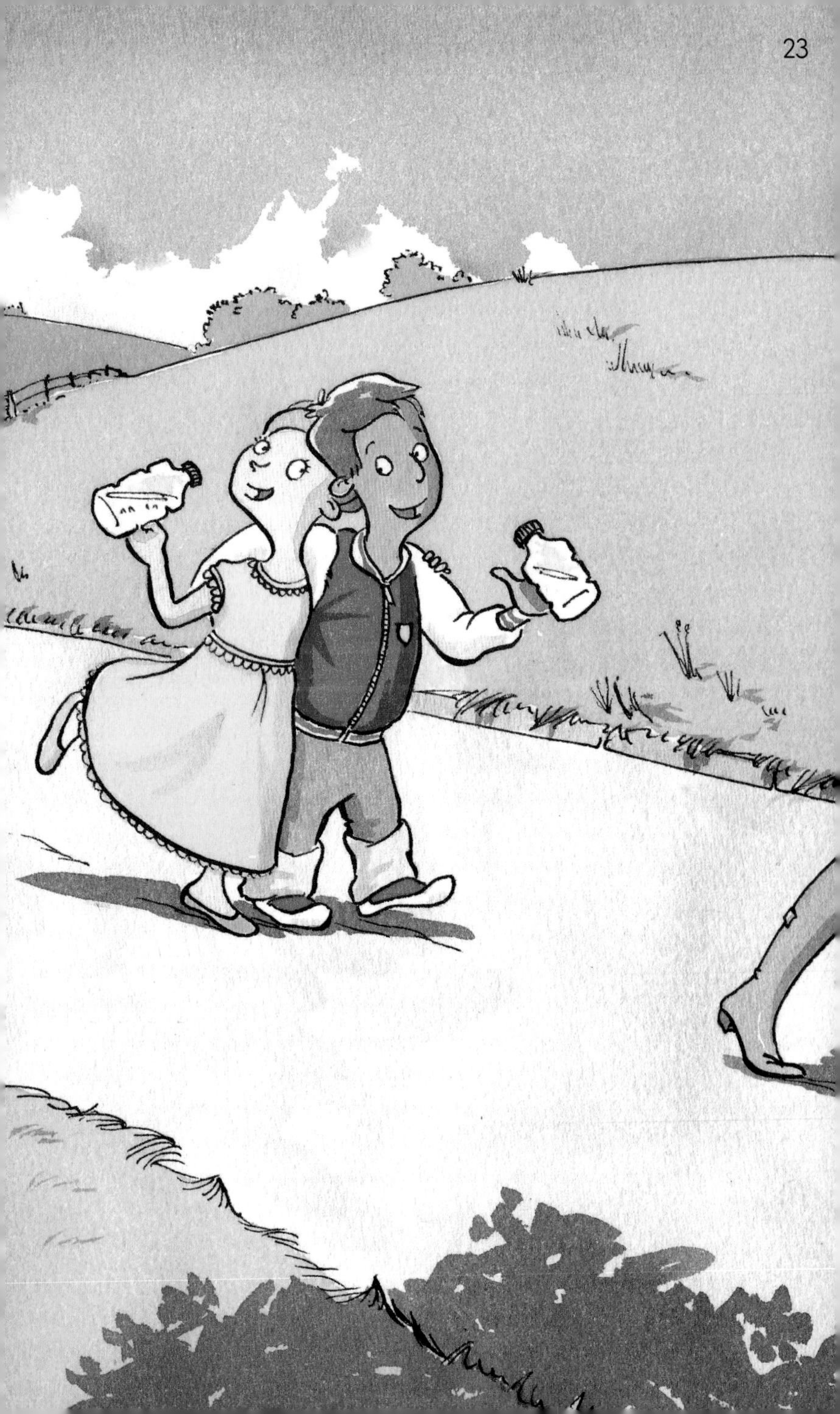

OVER **48** TITLES IN SIX LEVELS
Abigail Steel recommends...

Other titles to enjoy from Level 3

I love reading phonics **Bart's Go-Cart**

978-1-84898-552-0

I love reading phonics **Queen Ella's Feet**

978-1-84898-398-4

I love reading phonics **Puff Flies**

978-1-84898-399-1

Some titles from Level 1

I love reading phonics **Bad Rat**

978-1-84898-277-2

I love reading phonics **The Best Gift**

978-1-84898-396-0

I love reading phonics **Clint and Grant Play I-Spy**

978-1-84898-548-3

I love reading phonics **Gran and Bret's Trip**

978-1-84898-547-6

Some titles from Level 2

I love reading phonics **Wish Fish**

978-1-84898-386-1

I love reading phonics **Chuck and Duck**

978-1-84898-387-8

I love reading phonics **Pink Bunny**

978-1-84898-550-6

I love reading phonics **Let's go to the Swings**

978-1-84898-549-0

An Hachette UK Company
www.hachette.co.uk

Copyright © Octopus Publishing Group Ltd 2012
First published in Great Britain in 2012 by TickTock, a division of Octopus Publishing Group Ltd,
Endeavour House, 189 Shaftesbury Avenue, London WC2H 8JY.
www.octopusbooks.co.uk

ISBN 978 1 84898 551 3

Printed and bound in China
10 9 8 7 6 5 4 3 2 1